This book is dedicated to my mother.
When I was thirteen years old, I told her I wanted to be a photographer.
"Photography?" she gasped. "There's no money in that, son."
I've been a professional photographer since 1978!

Starting as a press photographer on local newspapers, I became a freelance in 1982,
working for magazines, newspapers and PR companies.

Along the way I picked up a lovely new camera, the Olympus XA,
and began to take it everywhere I went. Its discreet shutter and small size meant
it was ideal for surrepticious documentary photography, and I began to compile an
archive of what's popularly known now as 'street photography'

There was no 'plan' to this work.
I didn't commit to a 'project' like the majority of 'known' photographers did.
(Mainly because I didn't know that's what they did!)
I simply walked the streets of Manchester and my home town of Eccles,
practising how to become a photographer.
I hope you enjoy the results.

Martin

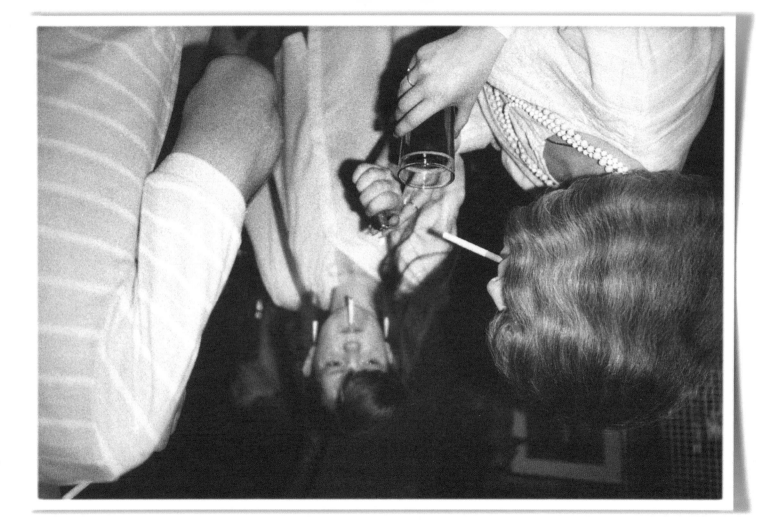

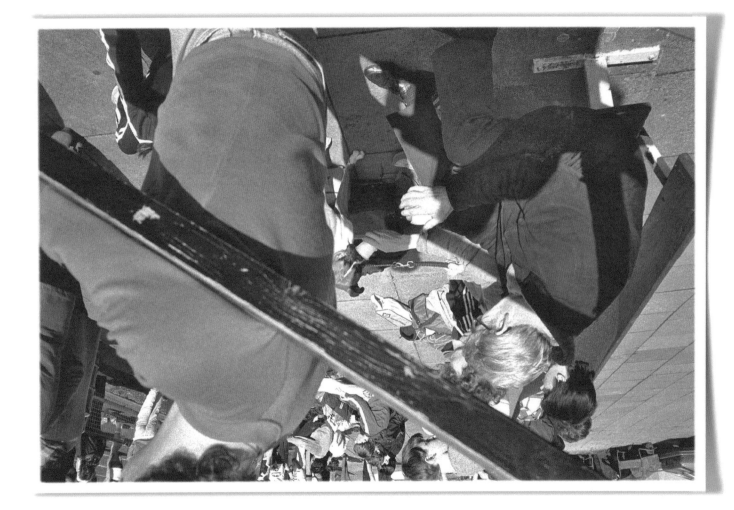

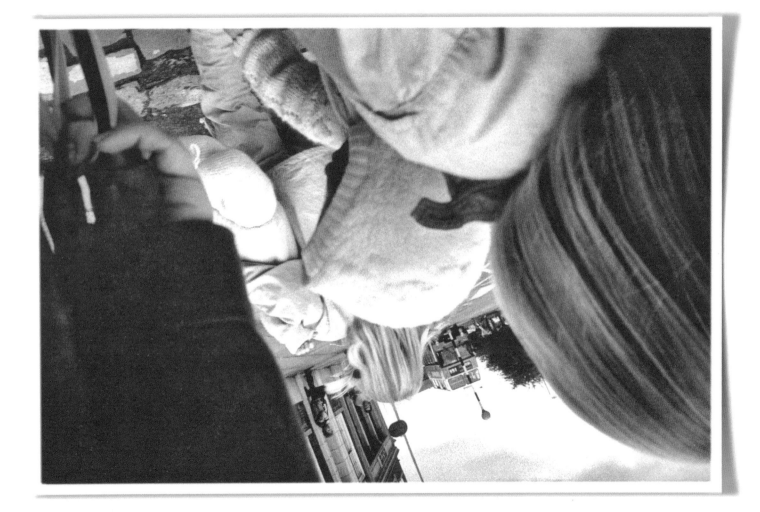

The Photographs

Cover - Two boys, Salford

1 - Manchester Art Gallery
2 - Teddy boys, Winton, Eccles
3 - Waitress, Buile Hill Hall, Salford
4 - Woman smoking, St. Peter's Square, Manchester
5 - Disco, Manchester
6 - Train to Manchester
7 - Morrison's Supermarket, Eccles
8 - The Conti Club, Manchester
9 - Outside Salford University
10 - Clarendon Leisure Centre, Salford
11 - Eccles Precinct
12 - Kids on Foxhill Road, Brookhouse Estate
13 - Book shop, John Dalton Street, Manchester
14 - Girl with doll, Church Street, Eccles
15 - Fish fingers - Grocer's store, Eccles
16 - Barton Air Show
17 - Man fixes car, Wagon & Horses pub car-park, Eccles
18 - Statue & air vent, Buile Hill Hall, Salford
19 - Morrison's Supermarket, Eccles
20 - Doddington Lane, Salford
21 - Meat delivery, Liverpool Road, Peel Green, Eccles
22 - My Dad, Alexandra Road, Eccles
23 - Woman cleans steps, New Lane, Eccles
24 - Foodsave store, Eccles
25 - Turner's chip shop, Peel Green, Eccles
26 - Passport machine, Eccles precinct
27 - Bus stop, Manchester
28 - Barton Lane, Eccles
29 - Gratrix Lane, Sale
30 - Fast-food van, Barton Air Show, Eccles
31 - Bus, Eccles
32 - Morrison's Supermarket, Eccles
33 - Morrison's Supermarket, Eccles
34 - Old Folks' Christmas meal, Salford
35 - Cyclist, The Crescent, Salford
36 - Timm's Tools, Patricroft, Eccles
37 - Road works, Liverpool Road, Eccles
38 - Lollypop Man, Liverpool Road, Eccles
39 - Music festival, Heaton Park, Manchester
40 - Retirement at school, (St. Gilbert's?), Eccles
41 - Liverpool Road, Eccles
42 - Turner's chip shop, Eccles
43 - Longford Park, Stretford
44 - Eccles precinct
45 - Church Street, Eccles
46 - Piccadilly Bus Station, Manchester
47 - Manchester Town Hall
48 - Bridge Street, Warrington
49 - Charity shop, Church Street, Eccles
50 - Eccles precinct
51 - Night club, Manchester
52 - Talk of the North night club, Eccles
53 - The Bridgewater pub, Eccles
54 - Punk gig, Manchester
55 - Oldham art gallery
56 - Bus window graffiti

And there's more ..

Book Two: Snaps? I'm an artist!
Book Three: So what do you do in the week?
Book Four: My Uncle's got a good camera
Book Five: Shot anyone famous?
Book Six: Who d'ya think you are, David Bailey ..?

All images available as A4 inkjet prints - £25
(Larger prints on request)

Contact Martin at moneill876@orange.fr

ISBN: 9798377361022

Wrong Way Wround Books

Printed in Great Britain
by Amazon